Karen's Magician

Look for these
and other books about Karen
in the
Baby-sitters Little Sister series:

1 Karen's Witch
2 Karen's Roller Skates
3 Karen's Worst Day
4 Karen's Kittycat Club
5 Karen's School Picture
6 Karen's Little Sister
7 Karen's Birthday
8 Karen's Haircut
9 Karen's Sleepover
#10 Karen's Grandmothers
#11 Karen's Prize
#12 Karen's Ghost
#13 Karen's Surprise
#14 Karen's New Year
#15 Karen's in Love
#16 Karen's Goldfish
#17 Karen's Brothers
#18 Karen's Home Run
#19 Karen's Good-bye
#20 Karen's Carnival
#21 Karen's New Teacher
#22 Karen's Little Witch
#23 Karen's Doll
#24 Karen's School Trip
#25 Karen's Pen Pal
#26 Karen's Ducklings
#27 Karen's Big Joke
#28 Karen's Tea Party
#29 Karen's Cartwheel
#30 Karen's Kittens
#31 Karen's Bully
#32 Karen's Pumpkin Patch
#33 Karen's Secret

#34 Karen's Snow Day
#35 Karen's Doll Hospital
#36 Karen's New Friend
#37 Karen's Tuba
#38 Karen's Big Lie
#39 Karen's Wedding
#40 Karen's Newspaper
#41 Karen's School
#42 Karen's Pizza Party
#43 Karen's Toothache
#44 Karen's Big Weekend
#45 Karen's Twin
#46 Karen's Baby-sitter
#47 Karen's Kite
#48 Karen's Two Families
#49 Karen's Stepmother
#50 Karen's Lucky Penny
#51 Karen's Big Top
#52 Karen's Mermaid
#53 Karen's School Bus
#54 Karen's Candy
#55 Karen's Magician
#56 Karen's Ice Skates

Super Specials:
1 Karen's Wish
2 Karen's Plane Trip
3 Karen's Mystery
4 Karen, Hannie, and
    Nancy: The Three
    Musketeers
5 Karen's Baby
6 Karen's Campout

Little Sister

Karen's Magician
Ann M. Martin

Illustrations by Susan Tang

A
LITTLE APPLE
PAPERBACK

SCHOLASTIC INC.
New York Toronto London Auckland Sydney

No part of this publication may be reproduced in whole or in part, or stored in a retrieval system, or transmitted in any form or by any means, electronic, mechanical, photocopying, recording, or otherwise, without written permission of the publisher. For information regarding permission, write to Scholastic Inc., 555 Broadway, New York, NY 10012.

ISBN 0-590-48230-0

12 11 10 9 8 7 6 5 4 3 2 1   4 5 6 7 8 9/9

Printed in the U.S.A.   40

First Scholastic printing, November 1994

*The author gratefully acknowledges
Stephanie Calmenson
for her help
with this book.*

Karen's Magician

Big House Saturday

"One, two, three, jump!" I called.

It was the first Saturday in November. I was playing with my little brother, Andrew. (He is four going on five.)

I jumped into a pile of bright crunchy leaves. I sank down to the bottom. When I climbed out again, I was covered with leaves from head to toe.

"I am the crunchy leaf monster!" I said. "I am coming to get you."

I flapped my arms and chased Andrew around the yard. Soon all the leaves flew

off. I was not a crunchy leaf monster any-more. I was just me — Karen Brewer.

Here are some things you might like to know about me. I am seven years old. I have blonde hair, blue eyes, and a bunch of freckles. I wear glasses, too. I have a blue pair for reading. I have a pink pair for the rest of the time.

"Karen! Andrew! Lunch is ready," called my big stepsister, Kristy.

"We are on our way," I replied.

Saturday lunch at the big house is one of my favorite meals. All the leftovers from the week go out on the kitchen table. Then everyone lines up with a plate and takes whatever they want. I was going to take a little of everything. Being a leaf monster was hard work. I was hungry.

Andrew and I lived at our little house in October. This was our first big-house week-end in a month. (I will tell you more about our two houses later.) We had a lot of catch-ing up to do.

"Shannon hurt her paw and had to go to

the veterinarian last week," said David Michael.

David Michael is my stepbrother. He is seven, like me. Shannon is his big, goofy puppy.

"What happened?" I asked.

"He stepped on a nail in the yard. He had to get a shot and wear a bandage for three whole days. But he is all better now."

"I am glad," I said.

"Elizabeth and I are going to the supermarket in a little while," said Daddy. (Elizabeth is my stepmother.) "Whoever is going to be home for supper gets to vote on dessert."

"All those who want chocolate ice cream, raise your hand," said Elizabeth.

I raised my hand.

"All those who want vanilla ice cream, raise your hand," said Elizabeth.

I raised my hand again. That is because I like both flavors.

"You only get one vote, Karen," said Daddy.

I picked chocolate.

"The vote is split down the middle," said Elizabeth. "We will get chocolate *and* vanilla."

Hurray!

We vote all the time at the big house. That is because there are so many of us. There are ten people, counting Andrew and me. So it is important to be organized.

That is just one interesting thing about the big house. There are interesting things about the little house, too.

So I will tell you all about my two houses.

Two Interesting Families

I used to live in one house. That was when I was little. Andrew and I lived with Mommy and Daddy at the big house in Stoneybrook, Connecticut. (Daddy grew up in the big house.)

But Mommy and Daddy started fighting a lot. It was awful. Mommy and Daddy thought so, too. So even though they love Andrew and me very much, they decided to get a divorce from each other.

Mommy moved with Andrew and me to our little house. Then she met a nice man named Seth. Mommy and Seth got married. Now Seth is our stepfather. Every other month Andrew and I live at the little house with Mommy, Seth, Rocky (Seth's cat), Midgie (Seth's dog), Emily Junior (my pet rat), and Bob (Andrew's hermit crab).

After the divorce, Daddy stayed at the big house. He met somebody new, too. Her name is Elizabeth. She and Daddy got married. That is how Elizabeth got to be our stepmother. She had four children from her first marriage. They are Kristy (she is thirteen and the best stepsister ever); David Michael (I already told you he is seven like me); and Sam and Charlie (they are so old they are in high school).

The next thing that happened was that Daddy and Elizabeth adopted Emily Michelle. She came from a faraway country called Vietnam. She is my adopted stepsister. She is two and a half and I love her very much. That is why I named my pet rat after her.

Nannie is Elizabeth's mother. She came

to live with us to help take care of Emily Michelle. Nannie is my stepgrandmother. I love her a lot.

I guess that is all. No, wait. I forgot to tell you about the pets at the big house. I told you about Shannon, David Michael's puppy. And Emily Junior and Bob live at the big house when Andrew and I are there. But there are also Boo-Boo (Daddy's cranky old tiger cat), Crystal Light the Second (my goldfish), and Goldfishie (Andrew's you-know-what).

So now you know how Andrew and I got to have two houses and two families. We have two of lots of other things also. I have two bicycles (one at each house), and Andrew has two tricycles. We have two sets of toys and books. We have two sets of clothes and shoes. I have two pieces of Tickly, my special blanket. I have two stuffed cats. (Moosie lives at the big house. Goosie lives at the little house.) I even have two best friends. Hannie Papadakis lives across the street and one house down from

Daddy's house. Nancy Dawes lives next door to Mommy's house. We are in the same second-grade class at Stoneybrook Academy. We call ourselves the Three Musketeers.

Andrew and I are lucky we can have two of so many things. It makes going back and forth much easier. It is also the reason we get to have special names. The special names I gave us are Karen Two-Two and Andrew Two-Two. (I got the idea for those names from a book my teacher, Ms. Colman, read to our class. The book was called *Jacob Two-Two Meets the Hooded Fang*.)

Now you know all about my two families. I told you they were interesting, didn't I?

Mr. Wizard

I woke up in my room at the big house. I got out of bed and looked at the calendar on my wall. It was the second Saturday of November.

"Yippee!" I said to Moosie. "Today is the day of the magic show."

Daddy was taking Andrew, David Michael, and me to Stamford, Connecticut, to see an exciting show. There were big advertisements in all the newspapers in town. They said:

Presto! Change-o!
Mr. Wizard Will Amaze You With
His Most Exciting Magic Show Ever!

I got dressed fast and went downstairs. Andrew was already in the kitchen. He had his magic trick set on the table. Andrew just loves magic.

He waved his wand across his bowl of cereal.

"Watch me make this cereal disappear," said Andrew.

He put his spoon in the bowl and started eating. Soon it was all gone.

"See? Magic," said Andrew. He had a big grin on his face.

We left to go to the show right after breakfast. It was at the Stamford Theater.

"I wonder if he is going to pull a rabbit out of his hat," said David Michael when we got there.

"I bet he will," said Andrew. "I bet Mr. Wizard can do anything."

The lights in the theater dimmed. The

11

curtain opened slowly. Puffs of orange and yellow smoke swirled around the stage. Out of the smoke, a man appeared. He was wearing a black cape and black magician's hat.

"Welcome, girls and boys, ladies and gentlemen. I am Mr. Wizard," he said.

Mr. Wizard tipped his hat. A white dove flew out. It settled on Mr. Wizard's arm.

Mr. Wizard waved a handkerchief in front of the dove. When he pulled the handkerchief away, the dove was blue. Then he waved his magic wand. The dove disappeared.

"Wow!" said Andrew.

Suddenly a table rose up from the center of the stage. On the table was a tank filled with water.

"I will need to borrow a few things from the audience," said Mr. Wizard. "When I point to you, please bring up a pen, a ring, or a penny if you have one. You will get it back at the end of the show."

I sat up tall. I wanted Mr. Wizard to point

to me. I was wearing the ring that came in my cereal box last week. It would be perfect for a magic trick.

Mr. Wizard was looking in our direction. Goody. He was pointing. I was about to stand up.

Then Mr. Wizard said, "Young man in the green shirt. Have you a penny for me?"

Mr. Wizard was not pointing to me. He was pointing to Andrew. Andrew jumped up and waved a penny in the air. He started to walk up to the stage.

"Andrew, wait," I whispered. "Isn't that your special souvenir penny? Isn't it the one that got flattened by the railroad train?"

"Don't worry," said Andrew. "Mr. Wizard promised to give it back."

Andrew was beaming as he walked onto the stage. Mr. Wizard called two more people from the audience.

"Please drop your objects into the tank," said Mr. Wizard. "Then watch what happens."

Right before our eyes, the objects dis-

appeared. But that was not all. They turned into goldfish!

"Did you see that? It was amazing!" said Andrew when he got back to his seat.

Andrew was right. Mr. Wizard's magic was truly amazing.

The Vanishing Penny

"Bravo!" "Hurray!" "Yippee!"

The audience clapped and cheered for Mr. Wizard when the show ended.

"Who wants to go to the Rosebud Cafe for lunch?" asked Daddy.

"I do!" I replied.

"Me, too," said David Michael.

"Can we get my penny back first?" asked Andrew.

I had forgotten all about Andrew's souvenir penny. Mr. Wizard said he would give it back. But where was Mr. Wizard?

"Let's go backstage," said Daddy. "We should be able to find Mr. Wizard there. He must have just forgotten to return it to you, Andrew."

We went up some stairs, then down a long hallway. A lady was standing outside Mr. Wizard's dressing room.

"We would like to see Mr. Wizard," said Daddy. "We would like to get my son's penny. It is a special souvenir penny."

"I am sorry," said the lady. "Mr. Wizard is not seeing anyone right now."

"That is okay," said Andrew. "Mr. Wizard *can't* give my penny back anyway."

"Why? Do you think he wants to keep it?" I asked.

"I think he does not *have* my penny anymore. He does not have the pen or the ring either," said Andrew. "They vanished. That is because Mr. Wizard is magic, *real* magic."

"I am sure Mr. Wizard has your penny," said Daddy. "I will write and ask him to please send it back."

We drove to the Rosebud Cafe. Andrew would not stop talking about Mr. Wizard's magic. He was sure his penny was gone forever.

We ate our lunch. Then we had a special treat. We got ice cream sundaes for dessert. I thought Andrew had forgotten about his penny by then. But when the waiter gave Daddy his change, there were three pennies in it. Andrew started talking about his penny again. He talked about it all the way home.

"Where does magic make a thing go?" asked Andrew. "Where *is* my penny?"

"Mr. Wizard has your penny," said Daddy. "He was just very good at tricking us into thinking it was gone."

"But Mr. Wizard sawed a man in half. He made a lady float in the air. So he could make my penny disappear, too," said Andrew. "It is *gone*. I know it is."

"Andrew, you have a book of magic tricks. You see how tricks work," said Daddy.

18

"The tricks in my book are easy tricks. They are kid tricks," said Andrew. "They are not real magic."

"We will get your penny back for you, Andrew," said Daddy. "I promise."

Andrew did not believe him. Before we went into the house, Andrew whispered in my ear, "My penny is *gone*."

Ms. Colman's Announcement

It was Monday morning. Hannie and I were waiting at the school bus stop.

"Here comes the bus," called Linny. (Linny is Hannie's brother. He is nine going on ten.)

The bus doors swished open and we climbed on. Hannie and I went to sit at the back with the other kids our age.

The big kids sit up front. That is because some of them used to be bullies. Now, Jack, the bus driver, watches them. So riding on the bus is fun.

Hannie and I played three games of tic-tac-toe and one game of dots. The next thing we knew, we were pulling up to our school.

"Hi, Nancy!" I called out the window.

Nancy was on the playground waiting for us. The Three Musketeers walked into our classroom together. Ms. Colman came in behind us.

"Please take your seats, everyone," said Ms. Colman. "We have a lot to do this morning."

Hannie and Nancy went to their desks at the back of the room. I used to sit at the back, too. But when I got glasses, Ms. Colman moved me up front. She said I could see better there. I think she was right.

There are two other kids who wear glasses and sit up front. They are Natalie Springer and Ricky Torres. (Ricky is my pretend husband. We got married on the playground at recess one day.)

"Karen, would you like to take attendance?" asked Ms. Colman.

21

"Sure," I replied.

I stood by Ms. Colman's desk. I quickly checked off me, Hannie, Nancy, Ricky, and Natalie. I looked around the room to see who else was there. Addie Sydney. Check. She was scraping a sticker off her wheelchair tray. Pamela Harding. Check. She is sometimes my best enemy. She was passing a note to her friends. There was one for Jannie Gilbert. Check. And one for Leslie Morris. Check. Audrey Green was there. Check. She once tried to be my twin. She dressed and acted exactly like me. I was glad she did not want to do that anymore. Terri Barkan. Check. Tammy Barkan. Check. They are twins for real. Bobbi Gianelli. Check. He is a sometimes bully. Hank Reubens. Check. Chris Lamar. Check. I kept going till I had checked off all the names.

"Everyone is here," I said.

"That is good," said Ms. Colman. "We are going to begin a new class project today. There is a very important day at the beginning of November. That day is Election Day. We are going to have our own elections in class."

"All right!" I called out.

"Indoor voice, please, Karen," said Ms. Colman. "And no calling out."

"Sorry," I replied. (Whenever I get too loud, Ms. Colman reminds me to use my indoor voice.)

"In the middle of December, our school is going to hold a Fun Night. We will have entertainment. We will sell tickets to raise money for our school," Ms. Colman explained.

I felt like shouting out, "Hurray!" But I did not do it. I shouted to myself so no one would hear me.

"There will be a Fun Night Committee," continued Ms. Colman. "Each grade will elect a representative for the committee."

I raised my hand. Ms. Colman called on me.

"I would like to be the representative," I said.

"Whoever would like to be the representative, please let me know tomorrow. We will hold elections in a few weeks. This will be a good way for us to learn about the election process. We will learn about campaigning. We will learn about voting."

I was way ahead of Ms. Colman. I was already planning my acceptance speech.

Andrew's Worry

"Would you like some more tea?" I said to Hannie.

"Thank you. I would love some," Hannie said.

The Three Musketeers were in my room at the big house. We were having a tea party. We were also having a serious talk about elections. Just like real grown-up ladies.

"If I win the election, I will have a lot of ideas for Fun Night. I know everything about having fun," I said.

"Nancy, are you going to run?" asked Hannie.

"I have not decided yet," said Nancy. "How about you?"

Hannie took a tiny sip of her tea. (It was really apple juice.)

"No. I do not think I will run," said Hannie. "I do not like so much attention. I do not like to be the center of things."

Knock knock.

Andrew poked his head into my room. He had a worried look on his face.

"Karen, where do you think my penny went?" he asked. "Is it even in this world anymore?"

"I think Mr. Wizard has it," I said. "Daddy told us Mr. Wizard is very good at tricks. Remember?"

"I think Mr. Wizard is very good at magic," said Andrew. "He made my penny disappear. I wonder where things go when they disappear by magic."

He closed the door behind him. We went back to our tea party.

"I just cannot decide. Should I run? Or should I not run?" asked Nancy.

"We could run together," I said. "It would be fun."

"I am not sure about that. One of us would have to win. The other would have to lose. I would not like that," said Nancy.

"You should run if you want to," I said. "We will still be friends."

"Maybe," said Nancy. "But maybe . . ."

Knock knock. It was Andrew again.

"If my penny did disappear, could *I* disappear, too?" asked Andrew. "I could go where my penny is. I could bring it back."

Poor Andrew. He could not stop worrying about his missing penny.

"I do not think that pennies or people disappear into thin air," I said. "Daddy will get your penny back for you. You will see."

Andrew closed the door behind him.

"I have decided not to run," said Nancy. "I do not want to run against my best friend. And I do not want to be on the committee as much as you do."

"I will help you in the election, Karen," said Hannie.

"Me too," said Nancy.

"Thank you," I replied

We put our hands together.

"One for all and all for one," we said.

When Hannie and Nancy left, I went outside to wait for Daddy to come home from work.

"Andrew came into my room twice," I said. "He is worried about his penny. I told him you would get it back for him."

"Thank you for reminding me," said Daddy. "I will see what I can do."

"I hope Mr. Wizard sends the penny back," I said. "If he does not, Andrew will never stop talking about it. Even when he is a very old man." I switched to my very old man's voice. "Where is my penny?" I said. "Has anyone seen my missing penny?"

Daddy laughed. "I will do my best to get it back. I promise."

Election Rules

It was Tuesday morning. I was at the back of the room talking with Hannie and Nancy when Ms. Colman walked in.

"Good morning, class," said Ms. Colman. "Everyone, please take your seats."

"See you later," I said. I raced to the front of the room.

It was Ricky's turn to take attendance. When he finished he said, "Everyone is here, Ms. Colman."

"Excellent," Ms. Colman replied. "We have a lot to do. This morning we will make a list of those of you who would like to run for representative of the second grade. Please remember that even if you win our class election, you still may not get to be the second-grade representative. The winner in our class will have to run against the winner in Mr. Berger's second-grade class."

Mr. Berger's second-grade class is next door to ours.

"Those of you who would like to run, please raise your hand," said Ms. Colman. "Karen, would you write the names down?"

I love doing important jobs for Ms. Colman. I took out my hot pink pen. That would make the list look gigundoly beautiful. I wrote my name in big letters at the top of the page.

These are the other kids who wanted to run: Pamela, Jannie, Hank, Chris. I wrote each of their names on the list.

I turned to look at Hannie and Nancy. I knew they were wondering the same thing

I was. How would Pamela and Jannie run against each other? Would one of them feel bad if the other won? I was glad I was not going to have that problem with my friends.

"We need to have some rules for the candidates to follow," said Ms. Colman. "I will start by writing three rules on the blackboard. Then I will ask if you can think of any others."

Here are Ms. Colman's rules:

Rule #1: You may spend up to five dollars on campaign supplies.

Rule #2: You may campaign before and after school, and during recess. No campaigning during class time.

Rule #3: No bribes allowed. This means you may not buy votes.

"Can anyone give me an example for rule number three?" asked Ms. Colman.

Hank raised his hand.

"We cannot give candy to kids so they will vote for us," he said.

"That is a very good example," said Ms.

Colman. "Now would anyone like to add a rule to our list?"

I raised my hand. Ms. Colman called on me.

"We are not allowed to make promises we cannot keep," I said.

"That sounds good," said Ms. Colman. "Will you give us an example?"

It took a minute. But I thought of a very good one.

"I should not promise to raise a million dollars if I am elected because I do not really think I could do it," I said.

"Excellent," said Ms. Colman.

She wrote on the board:

Rule #4: No false promises.

We decided that four rules would be enough to start. We would add more rules if we needed them later.

"All right then, class," said Ms. Colman. "Campaigning will start on Monday."

Morbidda Destiny

I worked on my campaign posters every day after school. By Saturday afternoon, I was ready for a break. I had plans to meet Hannie and Nancy at Morbidda Destiny's yard sale next door.

In case you did not know it, I think Morbidda Destiny is a witch. She swishes around in a black dress. She has a wart on her nose and hairs on her chin. I used to think it was scary living next door to a witch. But Morbidda Destiny is a nice witch.

"Look at this cute cup," said Hannie. "Maybe we should buy it for one of our tea parties."

The cup was black and white. It looked like a cat. The cat's tail curled up into a handle.

"That is a good cup for a witch's tea party," said Nancy. "But I do not think it is right for Lovely Ladies like us."

Just then, something interesting caught my eye.

"I will be right back," I said to Hannie and Nancy.

I hurried to a table at the other side of the yard. Leaning up against an old toaster was a big magic trick set. Guess what it was called. It was called *Mr. Wizard's Magic*.

I had to find Morbidda Destiny right away. I had to find out about that set.

"I got the set from my brother," said Morbidda Destiny when I asked her about it. "He is a famous magician. He calls himself Mr. Wizard."

Mr. Wizard was Morbidda Destiny's

brother. Wow! This was my chance. I told Morbidda Destiny about seeing her brother's magic show. I told her about Andrew's special penny.

"Do you think you could get the penny back for us? Andrew is really worried about it," I said.

"I would like to help you, Karen," said Morbidda Destiny. "But my brother is on the road with his show. I do not know how to reach him."

"May I look inside the box?" I asked.

"Of course," said Morbidda Destiny. "Everything is there. I checked it carefully this morning."

"Then I will be right back," I said. "Please do not let anyone else buy it. I am going to get some money. I am going to get Andrew, too."

In a flash, I was back at my house and knocking on Andrew's door.

I was happy I had enough money in my bank to buy Mr. Wizard's magic set. All I had to do next was show Andrew how Mr.

Wizard's fancy tricks worked. Then he would know his penny disappeared by tricks, not by magic.

I was knocking on Andrew's door. But no one was answering. I knocked harder.

"Come in," said Andrew finally.

I could tell by the sound of his voice that Andrew was worrying. I knew he was worrying about his penny. Have no fear, Karen is here, I thought. I opened the door to Andrew's room.

"Andrew, your worries are over," I said.

Real Magic

"Ta-daa! Here it is," I said.

I held up Mr. Wizard's magic trick set. I had made Andrew come to the yard sale to see it.

"Wait till you hear where Morbidda Destiny got this," I said. "She got it from Mr. Wizard. Mr. Wizard is her brother!"

"Oh, boy! Now we can find out where he is," said Andrew.

"I am afraid not," said Morbidda Destiny, coming out of nowhere. "As I told Karen, my brother is on the road. I do not

know how to reach him."

"That is okay," I said. "Everything I need to show Andrew is right in this box."

I handed Morbidda Destiny the money to pay for Mr. Wizard's magic trick set.

"I already have a magic trick set," said Andrew. "I do not need another one. I just want to see Mr. Wizard. I want to ask him if he will use his magic to bring my penny back."

"I told you there is no such thing as magic," I said. "Mr. Wizard uses tricks. Look."

I did not even wait to go into the house. I opened up the magic trick set in the yard. Hannie and Nancy came over to see it.

"Look at all those neat things," said Nancy.

There was a tall, black magician's hat. There was a wand. But most important, there were cards with instructions. The cards had everything you needed to know about magic tricks. There were even pictures.

"See? Mr. Wizard's show is *just tricks*," I said. "It is not real magic. Now do you believe me?"

"No," said Andrew. "Those tricks are for people who want to make believe they are magic. But Mr. Wizard really *is* magic."

"Andrew is right," said Morbidda Destiny. "My brother is real magic. He has been magic ever since he was a baby. Why, he even made his rattles disappear."

I could see a twinkle in Morbidda Destiny's eyes. I knew she was just kidding. But Andrew believed her.

"Wow! What else did he do?" asked Andrew.

"I am afraid I cannot tell. Those are family secrets," said Morbidda Destiny.

So much for my plan. Now Andrew would never believe me. Morbidda Destiny had ruined everything. Boo and bullfrogs. I wondered if I could get my money back.

The Fight

VOTE 4 KAREN

That was my motto. It was on all my campaign fliers. I wrote it in glitter. My fliers were sparkly.

It was Monday. Ms. Colman had not come into the room yet. So the candidates were allowed to campaign. I was handing out my fliers to all the kids in the class.

"I like your fliers, Karen," said Addie.

"Thank you. I like your new stickers," I said.

Addie was putting three new unicorn stickers on her wheelchair tray.

"Pamela gave them to me," said Addie. "Wasn't that nice of her?"

"It was very nice," I replied.

Hmm. Maybe it was *too* nice. Why was Pamela suddenly giving out stickers? It sounded like she was breaking rule number three: *No bribes allowed.*

Oh, well. At least *I* was not breaking any rules. I continued passing out my fliers. Hannie came over to help.

"Did you hear what Hank told Ricky?" she asked. "The whole class is talking about it."

"No, what?" I asked.

"Hank said his uncle is a talent scout. He said if he is elected he will get someone really famous to come to Fun Night."

"Oh, yeah?" I said.

Hmm. I wondered if Hank could really get someone famous to come to our school. If he could not, then he was breaking rule number four: *No false promises.*

Suddenly we heard raised voices at the back of the room. Pamela and Jannie were fighting.

"I did not take any of your dumb stickers," said Jannie. "You should not be handing them out anyway. You are buying votes."

"Yeah?" said Pamela. "Well, you spent more than five dollars on those fancy posters you made. But you won't win anyway. I am going to win this election."

Just then, Ms. Colman came into the room.

"I could hear shouting all the way down the hall," she said. "What is going on?"

Everyone turned to look at Pamela and Jannie.

"I do not want to run anymore," said Jannie. "I do not want to be in an election with Pamela." Then she turned to Pamela and said, "So there."

I was glad that the Three Musketeers were not running against each other. I did not think we would have a big fight like

Pamela and Jannie. But I did not want to take any chances.

"Pamela and Jannie, we will talk about this later," said Ms. Colman. "Now it is time for class to begin."

I sat down at my desk and put my fliers into my notebook. That is because rule number two said no campaigning during class.

The rule was not stopping Chris. He passed a note to Natalie. I peeked when she opened it. The note said: *Don't forget to vote for me! Your pal, Chris.*

Oh, well. At least one candidate had not broken any rules. Who was that candidate? Me. Karen Brewer. The candidate you can trust.

No Fair

"Step right up! Get your beautiful campaign buttons," I called.

It was Wednesday morning before class started. I was passing out my new campaign buttons. I had wanted to put my picture on the buttons. But that would have cost too much money. I wrote my motto on them instead.

"Nice campaign buttons, Karen," said Pamela, smiling. "I am going to hand my buttons out at lunchtime. I have one for you in case you decide not to run after all."

"You can keep your button, Pamela. I am definitely running," I said.

Now you see why Pamela is usually my best enemy.

As soon as Ms. Colman came in, I put my campaign buttons away.

"This morning we are going to talk about how real elections work," Ms. Colman said.

We learned that a candidate needs to share her ideas about important issues. That way voters can decide who to vote for.

I had good ideas about having fun. I had good ideas about raising money. I needed to tell the voters my ideas.

After lunch, I dragged a milk crate out to the playground. I turned it upside down and stood on it.

"Hear ye, hear ye," I called.

There was only one problem. Hannie and Nancy were the only ones paying any attention to me. The rest of the kids were crowded around Pamela.

"I will be right back," said Hannie. "I will see what Pamela is up to."

Hannie came back with one of Pamela's campaign buttons. Guess what was on the buttons. Pamela's picture! The kids thought her buttons were so great.

Then one by one the kids were crossing over to the other side of the playground. Chris was there.

"I will see what Chris is doing," said Nancy. "I will be right back."

Guess what Chris was handing out. Candy bars.

"I did not take any," said Nancy. "Even though they are my favorite kind."

"Thanks," I said.

I was starting to get upset. The other candidates were not following the rules. It was no fair.

I climbed down from my milk crate.

"Mind if I use this?" asked Hank.

Before I could answer, Hank was standing on the milk crate. *My* milk crate.

Suddenly the kids were crowding around Hank. Guess what he promised. He promised to get *two* superstars to come to the Fun Night.

I was running against fancy buttons. I was running against candy bars and superstars. I could tell the kids were starting to like the other candidates better than me. They were not even giving me a chance.

"Meeting at the monkey bars," I whispered to Hannie and Nancy.

We sat down under the monkey bars.

"What are we going to do?" asked Nancy. "Maybe we could think of a prize or something to hand out."

"Do you think you should drop out of the race?" asked Hannie.

"No way," I said. "I will not break the rules. And I will not drop out. I am going to stay in this race. And I am going to win. I will show them."

The class was going inside. I jumped up and ran to the playground door. I grabbed each kid's hand and shook it. (Important candidates always shake voters' hands.) I told the kids my ideas.

"Hey, Karen," said Natalie. "Chris is handing out more candy bars. Did you get one?"

I did not answer Natalie. I was too busy shaking hands.

Election Day

After lunch, Ms. Colman read a funny book to our class. It was called *The Boy Who Turned into a TV Set*. I was glad it was funny. I needed to be cheered up.

I had worked so hard on my campaign. But I did not think I had much chance to win the election. Maybe I could turn into a TV set. Maybe then the kids would vote for me.

As soon as the story was over, Ms. Colman handed out little slips of paper. I knew what that meant.

"It is time to hold our class election," Ms. Colman said. "I hope you have learned something about the election process during this week of campaigning. And I hope that you have remembered to follow the election rules. For example, I hope that no one has made any false promises."

Everyone turned to look at Hank. He was squirming in his seat.

"I hope no one has spent more than five dollars on the campaign," continued Ms. Colman.

Everyone turned to look at Pamela. Her face was bright red.

"And of course I hope no one has tried to buy any votes," said Ms. Colman.

Everyone looked at Chris. He buried his nose in a book.

I sat up tall. I might not win this election. But at least I did not have to hide. I turned and waved to Hannie and Nancy. They waved back.

"Please write down the name of the candidate you have chosen," said Ms. Colman.

"Then fold your paper in half and pass it to the front of the room. When you vote, I suggest you keep in mind the important ideas the candidates have shared with you."

I thought about my good ideas for Fun Night. I was sure I would be the best class representative. So I voted for myself. I knew that Hannie and Nancy would vote for me too. That made three votes.

I wondered if anyone else would vote for me. Ricky was my pretend husband. Maybe he would vote for me.

Ms. Colman wrote the names of the four candidates on the blackboard.

"Addie, would you please read the names on the slips of paper?" said Ms. Colman. "Bobby, please come up to the blackboard. It will be your job to put a check next to the names Addie calls out."

Addie unfolded the first piece of paper. She read the name.

"Karen Brewer," said Addie.

She unfolded another piece of paper.

53

"Karen Brewer," said Addie again.

Addie kept unfolding papers. She kept calling out my name. I could hardly believe it. I got almost every vote in the class. Only three kids did not vote for me. I knew who they were. Pamela. Hank. Chris.

"Congratulations, Karen," said Ms. Colman. "Do you have an acceptance speech prepared?"

I had written an acceptance speech a long time ago. But then I did not think I was going to win. So I had forgotten about the speech.

I did not let that stop me. I stood up and turned to the class.

"Thank you, thank you, thank you!" I said. "If I win the next election, I will try my best to be an excellent class representative."

I did it. I had won the election. I had won it honestly, too. I must really be a great campaigner.

Before I sat down I took a bow.

More Worries

I burst into the big house after school.

"I won! I won!" I cried.

"That is terrific," said Daddy.

"This calls for a celebration," said Elizabeth.

I decorated the kitchen with my extra campaign posters. I had extra campaign buttons, too. Everyone got to wear one at dinner.

While we ate, I told my family about the election.

"I am proud of you for running an honest campaign," said Daddy.

"You deserved to win," said Kristy.

For dessert, we had ice cream sundaes. Everyone was having a very good time at my election party. Everyone except Andrew. He looked worried.

"Do you want to play a game or something?" I said after dinner.

"No thanks. I am busy thinking," said Andrew.

"What are you thinking about?" I asked. (I already knew. But I asked anyway.)

"I am thinking about my penny," said Andrew. "I really need to know something. When a penny disappears *where does it go?*"

"Maybe we will find the answer in Mr. Wizard's magic trick set," I said.

Andrew had refused to play with the set since we got it. This time he agreed. (That is probably because I was an important elected official now.)

We went upstairs to the playroom and opened the box.

"You should wear this hat," I said.

I put the black magician's hat on Andrew's head.

Andrew looked through the box. I looked over his shoulder. There were card tricks, floating object tricks, pencil tricks.

"I see a vanishing penny trick," I said.

There was a handkerchief and a plastic penny to practice with.

I read the instructions. The magician was supposed to hold a penny underneath a handkerchief. The magician's helper would secretly take the penny away. The magician was supposed to pretend the penny was still there.

I read the end of the instructions out loud.

"After your helper has taken the penny, wave your arms in the air. Say, 'Prest-o! Change-o!' Flip the handkerchief over. Your audience will be amazed that the penny is gone," I said.

"So what?" said Andrew. "Mr. Wizard

did not do that trick. He did not have any helpers."

"Maybe he did not do this exact trick," I said. "But this is how he made your penny disappear. It was a trick. That is all."

"These are tricks," said Andrew. "Mr. Wizard is magic."

"I give up," I said. "If you want to think Mr. Wizard is magic, you go ahead. But I am an important elected official. I know better. I know it was a trick."

I also knew that Andrew did not believe me.

Vote 4 Karen

Before I went to sleep on Wednesday, I got my Vote 4 Karen buttons back from my family. I made a big stack of new posters, too.

I needed them for my campaign against Edwin Farley. He won the election in Mr. Berger's class. Now we had to run against each other.

On Thursday before school started, I asked Hannie and Nancy if they would help me hang my posters.

"Sure," said Hannie. "Where do you want them?"

"Everywhere!" I replied.

"Is that allowed?" asked Nancy.

"There is no rule about hanging posters," I said. "We just have to do it before class starts. Let's go."

By the time class started, Vote 4 Karen posters were hanging everywhere.

Ms. Colman was not very happy when she saw them.

"I know you did not break any rules, Karen," she said. "But I would like you to take some of those posters down."

I took down half of the posters. There were still a lot left.

I was not allowed to campaign again until recess. (Rule number two said no campaigning during class. Boo.)

When I finished eating, I carried my milk crate out onto the playground. I needed to share my ideas with the kids in Mr. Berger's class. I needed to make an important speech.

"Hear ye! Hear ye!" I called. "I, Karen Brewer, won the election in Ms. Colman's class. Did I run an honest campaign? Yes! Do I have excellent ideas for Fun Night? Yes! Should you vote for me for second-grade representative? Yes, yes, yes!"

"May I use the crate now?" asked Edwin.

"Um, I am not finished yet," I said. "If you want to make a speech, you should get your own milk crate."

I knew that was not very nice. But I needed to say a few more things. The only problem was, I could not think of any. So I just stood around for awhile.

Right after dinner on Thursday night I went upstairs to my room. I wanted to work on my campaign. I could not make any more buttons or posters. I had already spent five dollars.

"What should I do, Moosie?" I asked. "I know. I will make up a song. That does not cost anything."

Writing a campaign song was hard work. I had to write it and rewrite it. Finally it was ready. I sang my song to Moosie.

Vote for Karen. It is the best thing to do.
Vote for Karen. Let me represent you.
Vote for Karen. You will be voting for fun.
Vote for Karen. Hear me shout out, "I won!"

I could tell Moosie liked my song a lot. Tomorrow at recess, I would get on my milk crate. I would sing my song to everyone.

The election was going to be held in the afternoon. I was sure I would win by a landslide.

The Winner Is . . .

I did not get to sing my song on Friday. That is because I had to stay in at recess. Ms. Colman asked me to write one more speech.

"This will be your last chance to tell everyone why they should vote for you, Karen. If you need my help, just let me know."

"Thank you," I replied. "But I would like to do this by myself."

I finished writing just as the kids started coming back from recess. Mr. Berger's class carried their chairs into Ms. Colman's room.

"You can go first, Karen," said Edwin. "I did not finish my speech yet."

I walked to the front of the room. Uh-oh. I had forgotten something. I whispered in Ms. Colman's ear.

"No, Karen," Ms. Colman whispered back. "You do not need to stand on a milk crate. You are fine right where you are."

I felt a few butterflies fluttering in my stomach. But they settled down as soon as I started to talk.

"Hi. I am going to tell you why I think you should vote for me, Karen Brewer.

"First of all, I love being in second grade. And I am very proud of my school. So if you elect me, I will try my best to do a good job.

"Second, I have a lot of energy. I know that some people think I have *too* much energy. But energy is a good thing for a class representative to have.

"Both little kids and big kids will be on the Fun Night Committee. Sometimes big kids think they know everything. Sometimes they think they do not have to listen to second-graders. It will take a lot of energy to get them to listen.

"The last thing you should know about me is that I have good ideas about having fun. And I promise I will listen to *your* ideas too. Thank you."

Some of the kids clapped. But not everyone. I guess they were tired from recess.

"Thank you, Karen," said Ms. Colman. "You may take your seat. Edwin, would you like to come up now?"

I could see that most of what he had written down was crossed out. His speech was very short.

"Hi, my name is Edwin Farley. I promise to do a good job if I am elected. I want to be on the Fun Night Committee because my cousin, who is in fourth grade, is going to be on the committee, too. I think I have good ideas about having fun. Those are the reasons I think you should vote for me. Thank you."

"Thank you, Edwin," said Mr. Berger. "Now we are going to pass around voting slips. Please write the name of the candidate you choose. Then fold the paper and pass it to the front of the room."

Ms. Colman said it would take too long to read the names out loud. So two kids opened the slips of paper and counted the votes. The two kids were Audrey Green and Liddie Yuan. Liddie is in Mr. Berger's class.

They wrote the number of votes on a piece of paper and handed them to Ms. Colman.

"This was a very close race, class," said Ms. Colman. "Thank you Karen and Edwin for running a good and honest campaign."

Did I hear right? Did Ms. Colman say the race was close? I thought almost everyone would vote for me.

Ms. Colman passed the paper to Mr. Berger.

"The winner is Karen Brewer. Congratulations, Karen," said Mr. Berger.

I turned around and waved to everyone. But I did not get up and take a bow. I did not shout "yippee."

I had a feeling some kids in my class had not voted for me this time. I think some kids did not like it when I would not give the milk crate to Edwin. And some kids did not like it when I put up all those posters.

I guess I had overdone it a little. But at least I had won. I would work hard on the committee. I would make everyone proud.

The Meeting

On Monday morning, I woke up extra early.

"Today is an important day," I said to Moosie. "This afternoon, I am going to my first Fun Night Committee meeting."

I wanted to wear something special. I put on a blue skirt, blue tights, and blue shoes. I put on my blue-and-red-striped sweater. Then I put one red ribbon and one blue ribbon in my hair.

"That will show them I know how to have fun. Wish me luck, Moosie," I said.

The meeting was held after school. There was one representative from every grade. There were two teachers. They were Mr. Berger and Ms. Williams. (Ms. Williams is a fourth-grade teacher.)

"Fun Night will be held the first week in December," said Ms. Williams. "We need to decide the kind of entertainment we would like to have. If you have any suggestions, please raise your hand."

Two hands shot up right away. The fifth- and sixth-grade representatives already had ideas. I had an idea, too. But I decided to let the big kids talk first.

"I think we should have kids from our school in the show. We could hold auditions and pick the best performers," said the fifth-grader.

"That is a good idea," said Mr. Berger. "There is a lot of talent in our school. We can have music and dance performances."

"And we could have a stand-up comedian," said the third-grader.

"Robert, you had your hand raised. What

was your idea?" asked Ms. Williams. (Robert was the sixth-grader.)

"I was going to suggest that we get a professional performer," said Robert. "People will pay more to see a professional act. And we are trying to raise as much money as we can for the school."

"That is good thinking," said Ms. Williams. "All we have to do is decide what kind of performer to hire."

I knew a performer. A very good professional performer. That was the idea I had wanted to share before.

I was a little scared to raise my hand. But I had to. I just had to. I could not let the second grade down. I was there to represent them.

I raised my hand high enough to scratch my chin. I raised my hand a little more and tugged on my red ribbon. Finally I put my hand straight up in the air.

"Yes, Karen?" said Mr. Berger.

"Maybe we could get Mr. Wizard. He is

a really good magician. He could be our star attraction," I said.

"I saw Mr. Wizard's show. I went on my birthday," said Peggy, the first-grader. "It was fun."

"If the show was fun, then it will be perfect for our Fun Night," said Mr. Berger. "A show like that is good for all ages."

Everyone was excited about my idea. I got excited, too. I was not scared to speak up anymore.

"It may not be so easy to reach him," I explained. "I happen to know Mr. Wizard's sister. She says he is on the road now."

"You do not have to worry about that," said Ms. Williams. "Mr. Berger and I will work on lining up Mr. Wizard for our show."

"This was a very good meeting," said Mr. Berger. "You all did an excellent job."

I did it! I did an excellent job. And I had had fun.

Let's see. What else could I run for? Maybe I could run for president of the United States. I wonder if that job would be fun, too.

The Rehearsal

"Karen, it is time to get up," said Mommy.

It was the first Monday in December. Andrew and I were back at the little house with Mommy and Seth.

The beginning of the month was always kind of confusing. That is because I missed the people I had just left. But I was also happy to be where I was.

"I will be right down," I called.

Knock knock. Andrew poked his head in the door.

"Is he really coming?" asked Andrew. "Did he really promise?"

"Yes, he really promised to come," I replied.

The teachers had reached Mr. Wizard. He had agreed to perform at Stoneybrook Academy. Andrew was excited. He asked me about it every single day.

I looked at my calendar. Fun Night was only four days away. The Fun Night Committee had already held auditions. We had picked the best performers from our school. We were having a rehearsal at two o'clock.

During school that day, I had trouble paying attention. I was waiting for two o'clock. Waiting. Waiting. Finally two o'clock came.

"Karen, you may be excused for the Fun Night rehearsal," said Ms. Colman.

Yippee!

"Pamela, Jannie, and Leslie, you are also excused," said Ms. Colman.

Pamela, Jannie, and Leslie were going to

perform in the show. (Pamela and Jannie had made up after the election.) They had a silly act that made everyone laugh.

I wished the Three Musketeers were going to be in the show together. But I was too busy being second-grade representative. Nancy had been absent the day of the auditions. And Hannie did not want to be in the show without us.

I walked to the auditorium with Pamela, Jannie, and Leslie. They went backstage to wait for their turn to perform. I sat down to watch the show with the other committee members.

The first act was a performance by the Double Daredevils. They were two kids from the sixth grade.

"Please sit back and relax," said the Daredevils. "We will amaze you with our gymnastics skills."

They flipped and tumbled across the stage. They were very, very good.

Next came a comedian named Hilarious Hilary. She was in the fifth grade. Hilary told lots of funny jokes. She told them in funny voices. Here is my favorite one: What does a bumblebee with hiccups flying backward say? He says, "Zzub-zzub-hic! Zzub-zzub-hic!"

Then it was time for the Tongue Twister Sisters to perform. Guess who the Tongue Twister Sisters were. They were Pamela, Jannie, and Leslie.

They recited three tongue twisters together really fast. Then they said, "Whoever knows the next twister, please join in."

Here is the twister: *How much wood would a woodchuck chuck if a woodchuck could chuck wood? A woodchuck would chuck as much wood as a woodchuck could chuck, if a woodchuck could chuck wood!*

I knew that twister really well. I said it with them. I did not make one mistake.

Our rehearsal was over. It was great. Fun Night was going to be the best night of the year.

The Plan

Hannie invited Nancy and me to her house after school.

We made raisin toast with cream cheese for our snack. While we were eating, I told Hannie and Nancy one of Hilarious Hilary's jokes.

"Where do cows go on vacation?" I asked.

"I don't know," said Hannie. "Where?"

"*Moo* York," I replied. I mooed like a cow.

When we finished eating we did our

homework. Then Hannie said, "What should we do now?"

"Let's put on a show," said Nancy.

"We could put on a magic show," I said. "I will go to Daddy's and get Mr. Wizard's magic set. I am sure Andrew will not mind if we borrow it. I will be right back."

When I opened Hannie's front door, I saw a strange sight. An old green car with yellow fenders was parked in Morbidda Destiny's driveway. The license plate was 434MAGIC.

Guess who was walking up Morbidda Destiny's front steps. Mr. Wizard!

I thought of running back to tell Hannie and Nancy. But then I thought of something better. I thought of a plan. It was a plan to help Andrew.

I looked both ways. Then I crossed the street to the witch's house. Mr. Wizard was just about to ring the bell.

"Hi," I said. "My name is Karen Brewer. I live next door. Well, actually I live next door every other month. That is because my parents are divorced. So one month I live with my mother. And one month I live with my father. But that is not what I wanted to say."

I was a little bit nervous. That is why I was talking so much.

"I am pleased to meet you," said Mr. Wizard. "Is there something special you want to tell me?"

"As a matter of fact there is," I said. I told Mr. Wizard that Andrew and I had been at his show.

"I hope you enjoyed it," said Mr. Wizard.

"Oh, yes," I said. "We enjoyed it very much."

Then I told him how worried Andrew was about his penny.

"I am sorry to hear that," said Mr. Wizard.

Finally I told him my plan.

"Well," said Mr. Wizard. "I will see what I can do to help."

"Thank you, Mr. Wizard," I said.

Mr. Wizard shook my hand. Then I

waved good-bye and went next door to get the magic set. I hurried back to Hannie's house with it.

"What took you so long?" asked Nancy.

"Oh, nothing," I replied. I opened the box. "Who wants to wear the magician's hat?" I asked, waving it in the air.

I did not say a word about seeing Mr. Wizard. I did not say a word about my plan.

Fun Night

"Presto! Change-o! It is Fun Night," I said to Goosie. I was standing in front of the mirror admiring my outfit.

"Come on, Karen. Let's go," said Andrew. Andrew had been ready for hours.

I hurried downstairs so we would not be late.

When we got to school, my big house family was already there. Everyone from both my families had tickets to the show. But our seats were not together. I ran to hug Daddy and everyone from the big house. Then I sat with Mommy, Seth, and Andrew.

The lights in the room dimmed. Robert, the sixth-grader from our committee, introduced the show.

"Welcome to Stoneybrook Academy's Fun Night," he said. "Here are our first performers, the Kindergarten Kids."

The Kindergarten Kids sang and acted out *Farmer in the Dell*. At the end of the song the cheese ran away. The mouse ran after the cheese. The cat ran after the mouse. The dog ran after the cat. And that is how everyone got off the stage.

Hilarious Hilary, the Double Daredevils, and the Stoneybrook Rock 'n' Roll Band were the next acts. They were all great.

"Now please welcome the Tongue Twister Sisters," said Robert.

Pamela, Jannie, and Leslie came out and took a bow. They did very well until they tried to say Peter Piper picked a peck of pickled peppers. Their tongues got all twisted up.

"Peter Peeper piped a pippled pickle," they said.

They started giggling. Then laughing. Soon they were laughing so hard, they had to be led off the stage. They were as funny as Hilarious Hilary.

The curtains closed. Ms. Williams came out front. She talked to the audience about raising money for the school.

When she finished, Robert said, "And now for our star attraction. Please welcome Mr. Wizard and his amazing magic show!"

Just like before, puffs of orange and yellow smoke swirled around the stage. Out of the smoke, Mr. Wizard appeared.

"Welcome, girls and boys, ladies and gentlemen. I am Mr. Wizard," he said.

Mr. Wizard tipped his hat. Out jumped a rabbit.

Mr. Wizard showed us that the hat was empty. Then he put it over the rabbit. When he picked up the hat again, the rabbit was gone. Instead of the rabbit, there was a big bunch of carrots.

Mr. Wizard did lots of amazing tricks. Then he said, "I need two volunteers for the most amazing trick of all. One volunteer will be sawed in half. The other volunteer will be my special assistant."

Mr. Wizard picked a fifth-grade boy to be his first volunteer. Then he started looking for his second volunteer.

I tapped Andrew on the shoulder.

"Raise your hand," I whispered. "Maybe Mr. Wizard will pick you. You can be his special assistant."

"I don't know if I want to," said Andrew.

"Go on," I said. "It will be fun."

Andrew raised his hand. Mr. Wizard picked him. Everything was going according to my plan.

Andrew got to hold the magic saw. He even got to say "Presto! Change-o!" Right before our very eyes, we watched the fifth-grade boy get sawed in half.

The audience clapped and cheered.

"That was pretty neat magic," I said when Andrew came back to his seat.

Andrew did not say a word. He just looked at me and grinned.

Andrew's Secret

After the show, I went backstage with Mommy, Seth, and Andrew.

Mr. Wizard's door was open. But I knocked anyway before I walked in.

"Welcome, Karen. Welcome," said Mr. Wizard. "I see you brought your family with you. Your little-house family, that is."

I was very proud to have an important friend like Mr. Wizard. I introduced him to Mommy and Seth.

"And I guess you know Andrew already," I said.

"Of course," said Mr. Wizard. "Andrew was my best assistant ever."

I could see that Andrew felt proud, too.

"I know how Mr. Wizard saws people in half," Andrew said. "It is a trick. It is not real magic."

"It is an amazing trick," said Seth. "Do you really know how it is done, Andrew?"

"I know exactly how," Andrew replied. "Mr. Wizard showed me everything while I was helping him."

"That is very exciting," said Mommy.

"How is the trick done?" I asked.

Andrew squeezed his lips together. He made believe he was zipping them up. Andrew was not talking.

"I guess the trick is going to be Andrew's secret," said Mr. Wizard.

Hmm. This was not part of my plan. I wished Andrew would tell me the trick. Maybe he would tell me later. But on second thought, maybe I did not really want to know. I liked to be amazed by Mr. Wizard's show. If I knew the tricks, the show might not be so amazing.

There was just one more part of my plan left.

"Excuse me, Mr. Wizard," I said. "Didn't you say you wanted to pay Andrew for helping you out?"

Mr. Wizard was not really going to pay Andrew. But I thought it would be a good way of reminding him about our plan.

At first Mr. Wizard looked puzzled. Then he said, "Oh, yes, yes. You are right, Karen."

He reached into his pocket. He pulled out Andrew's souvenir penny.

"I am so sorry I forgot to return this to you, Andrew," said Mr. Wizard. "I can be very forgetful sometimes."

Andrew was happy to have his penny back. And I was happy that Andrew did not have to worry anymore. He finally knew that Mr. Wizard was not real magic.

He was just very good at tricks.

"Good night, Mr. Wizard. And thank you," I said.

"You are very welcome, Karen. Good night, everyone," said Mr. Wizard.

Suddenly there were great big puffs of orange and yellow smoke. Presto! Change-o! Mr. Wizard was gone.

About the Author

ANN M. MARTIN lives in New York City and loves animals, especially cats. She has two cats of her own, Mouse and Rosie.

Other books by Ann M. Martin that you might enjoy are *Stage Fright; Me and Katie (the Pest)*; and the books in *The Baby-sitters Club* series.

Ann likes ice cream and *I Love Lucy*. And she has her own little sister, whose name is Jane.

Little Sister

Don't miss #56

KAREN'S ICE SKATES

When I walked out the door, I saw Nancy coming toward me from one direction. Bobby Gianelli was coming from the other direction. Bobby's skates were hanging from his shoulder.

"Want to come see if the pond is ready?" asked Bobby.

"Okay!" said Nancy and I at the same time.

Maybe I should not have said yes so fast. After all, Grandad said the pond was not ready. But I only overheard him. He did not say anything to *me*. I could have heard him wrong when he was talking to Seth. Anyway, Grandad was a worrier. Maybe the ice really was ready. It would not hurt to look.

88888888₹LITTLE 🍎 APPLE₹88888888

BABY·SITTERS

Little Sister™

by Ann M. Martin, author of *The Baby-sitters Club*®

❏	MQ44300-3	#1	Karen's Witch	$2.95
❏	MQ44259-7	#2	Karen's Roller Skates	$2.95
❏	MQ44299-7	#3	Karen's Worst Day	$2.95
❏	MQ44264-3	#4	Karen's Kittycat Club	$2.95
❏	MQ44258-9	#5	Karen's School Picture	$2.95
❏	MQ44298-8	#6	Karen's Little Sister	$2.95
❏	MQ44257-0	#7	Karen's Birthday	$2.95
❏	MQ42670-2	#8	Karen's Haircut	$2.95
❏	MQ43652-X	#9	Karen's Sleepover	$2.95
❏	MQ43651-1	#10	Karen's Grandmothers	$2.95
❏	MQ43650-3	#11	Karen's Prize	$2.95
❏	MQ43649-X	#12	Karen's Ghost	$2.95
❏	MQ43648-1	#13	Karen's Surprise	$2.75
❏	MQ43646-5	#14	Karen's New Year	$2.75
❏	MQ43645-7	#15	Karen's in Love	$2.75
❏	MQ43644-9	#16	Karen's Goldfish	$2.75
❏	MQ43643-0	#17	Karen's Brothers	$2.75
❏	MQ43642-2	#18	Karen's Home-Run	$2.75
❏	MQ43641-4	#19	Karen's Good-Bye	$2.95
❏	MQ44823-4	#20	Karen's Carnival	$2.75
❏	MQ44824-2	#21	Karen's New Teacher	$2.95
❏	MQ44833-1	#22	Karen's Little Witch	$2.95
❏	MQ44832-3	#23	Karen's Doll	$2.95
❏	MQ44859-5	#24	Karen's School Trip	$2.95
❏	MQ44831-5	#25	Karen's Pen Pal	$2.95
❏	MQ44830-7	#26	Karen's Ducklings	$2.75
❏	MQ44829-3	#27	Karen's Big Joke	$2.95
❏	MQ44828-5	#28	Karen's Tea Party	$2.95

More Titles... 👉

The Baby-sitters Little Sister titles continued...

❑ MQ44825-0	#29	Karen's Cartwheel	$2.75
❑ MQ45645-8	#30	Karen's Kittens	$2.75
❑ MQ45646-6	#31	Karen's Bully	$2.95
❑ MQ45647-4	#32	Karen's Pumpkin Patch	$2.95
❑ MQ45648-2	#33	Karen's Secret	$2.95
❑ MQ45650-4	#34	Karen's Snow Day	$2.95
❑ MQ45652-0	#35	Karen's Doll Hospital	$2.95
❑ MQ45651-2	#36	Karen's New Friend	$2.95
❑ MQ45653-9	#37	Karen's Tuba	$2.95
❑ MQ45655-5	#38	Karen's Big Lie	$2.95
❑ MQ45654-7	#39	Karen's Wedding	$2.95
❑ MQ47040-X	#40	Karen's Newspaper	$2.95
❑ MQ47041-8	#41	Karen's School	$2.95
❑ MQ47042-6	#42	Karen's Pizza Party	$2.95
❑ MQ46912-6	#43	Karen's Toothache	$2.95
❑ MQ47043-4	#44	Karen's Big Weekend	$2.95
❑ MQ47044-2	#45	Karen's Twin	$2.95
❑ MQ47045-0	#46	Karen's Baby-sitter	$2.95
❑ MQ43647-3		Karen's Wish Super Special #1	$2.95
❑ MQ44834-X		Karen's Plane Trip Super Special #2	$3.25
❑ MQ44827-7		Karen's Mystery Super Special #3	$2.95
❑ MQ45644-X		Karen's Three Musketeers Super Special #4	$2.95
❑ MQ45649-0		Karen's Baby Super Special #5	$3.25
❑ MQ46911-8		Karen's Campout Super Special #6	$3.25

Available wherever you buy books, or use this order form.

- -

Scholastic Inc., P.O. Box 7502, 2931 E. McCarty Street, Jefferson City, MO 65102

Please send me the books I have checked above. I am enclosing $ _____ (please add $2.00 to cover shipping and handling). Send check or money order - no cash or C.O.Ds please.

Name _____ Birthdate _____

Address _____

City _____ State/Zip _____

Please allow four to six weeks for delivery. Offer good in U.S.A. only. Sorry, mail orders are not available to residents to Canada. Prices subject to change.

BLS793

Now THE BABY-SITTERS CLUB®

★ is a Video Club too! ★

THE BABY·SITTERS CLUB®

Stacey
Claudia
Krusty
Mallory's
Jessi
Dawn
Mary Anne

Wow! It's really them—
the new Baby-sitters Club dolls!

Your favorite Baby-sitters Club characters have come to life in these beautiful collector dolls. Each doll wears her own unique clothes and jewelry. They look just like the girls you have imagined! The dolls also come with their own individual stories in special edition booklets that you'll find nowhere else.

Look for the new Baby-sitters Club collection...
coming soon to a store near you!

Kenner®